# I
# Won't
# Quit

Written by
## Danny McGill

Illustrated by
## Sumit Roy

This book is dedicated to my beautiful niece Cady. Her kindness and compassion, her infectious smile and sense of humor, and her grit... These qualities made a difference to so many people. And we will hold Cady and her example in our hearts forever.

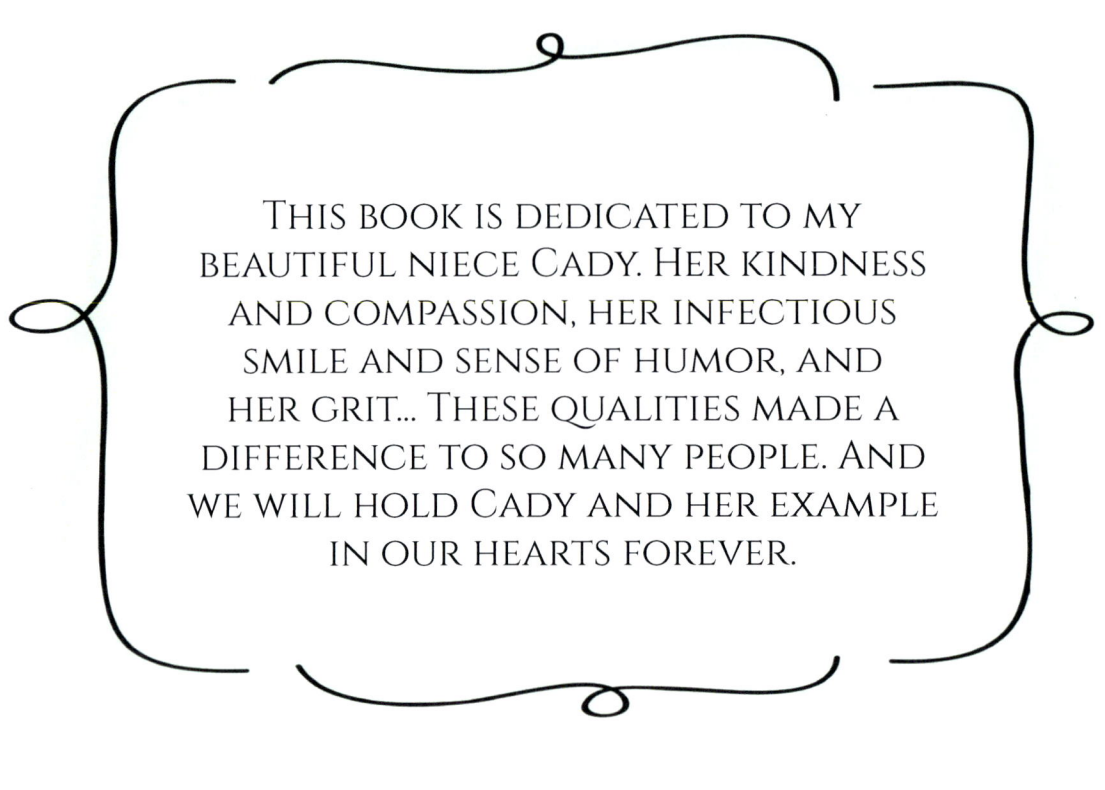

I could watch how other people tie their shoes.

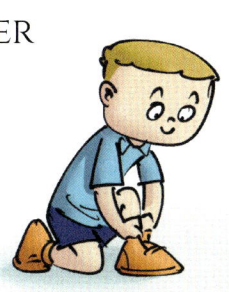

I could visit the Shoe Tying Institute of America.

I could practice with the shoelace box at school.

But no matter what, I won't quit.

Sometimes, I feel embarrassed when I can't ride my bike.

But I won't quit.

I could put on new training wheels.

I could ride my bike someplace really safe.

I could spend more time riding around the track near our house.

But no matter what, I won't quit.

Sometimes, I feel bored when I practice the piano.

But I won't quit.

I COULD TAKE MY SHOW ON THE ROAD.

I COULD JOIN A BAND.

I COULD GIVE MYSELF A REWARD EACH TIME I FINISH PRACTICING.

BUT NO MATTER WHAT, I WON'T QUIT.

Sometimes, I feel embarrassed when I can't hit a baseball.

But I won't quit.

I could replace the old baseball with one a little bigger.

I could let my big brother play for me during the next game.

I could spend extra time each day hitting balls off the tee.

But no matter what, I won't quit.

Sometimes, I feel annoyed when it's time to do chores around the house.

But I won't quit.

I could give my baby brother a lollipop for cleaning the dirty dishes.

I could hypnotize my dad into vacuuming the house.

I could watch Attack of the Killer Underwear while I fold the laundry.

But no matter what, I won't quit.

Sometimes, I feel frustrated when I have to do math homework.

But I won't quit.

I could tell my teacher that my brain accidentally got thrown away in the garbage.

I could ask a genie to magically finish my assignment.

I could carry flashcards wherever I go and get lots and lots of practice.

But no matter what, I won't quit.

Sometimes, I feel angry when my big brother beats me at board games.

But I won't quit.

I could replace his chess pieces with spiders and bugs.

I could distract him with the world's tallest ice cream cone.

I could study a book about how to win at chess.

But no matter what, I won't quit.

Sometimes, I feel miserable when my mom makes me go to swim practice.

But I won't quit.

I could drain all the water out of the swimming pool.

I could build a robot to go in my place.

I could practice swimming extra laps with my dad in the evenings.

But no matter what, I won't quit.

Sometimes, I feel scared when it's my turn to give a speech in front of the class.

But I won't quit.

I could hide behind a glass wall, so the rotten fruit won't hit me.

I could picture my classmates wearing silly paper bag masks.

I could practice in front of my mom and dad at home.

But no matter what, I won't quit.

Sometimes, I feel sad when I don't get much playing time on my basketball team.

But I won't quit.

I COULD SECRETLY TAKE OVER AS COACH OF THE TEAM.

I COULD WEAR THE TALLEST SHOES IN THE WORLD.

I COULD PRACTICE DRIBBLING AND SHOOTING EVERY DAY AFTER SCHOOL.

BUT NO MATTER WHAT, I WON'T QUIT.

Whether it's tying my shoes, riding a bike, learning an instrument, doing my homework, or playing on a team... no matter how hard it sometimes gets, I won't do it.

I just won't quit!

My name is John, and I'm Cady's dad. Sometimes I want to quit things too. Like my diet. Or my New Year's resolution to exercise more. Or the new project I've started at work. Or a commitment I've made to my family. I get busy. Things get hard. I get embarrassed. Or I get scared. But no matter what, I won't quit either.

Now you try! (You can even draw your own pictures.)

Do you ever feel like you want to quit something?
What could you do instead?

Sometimes I feel _____

when I _____.

But I won't quit.

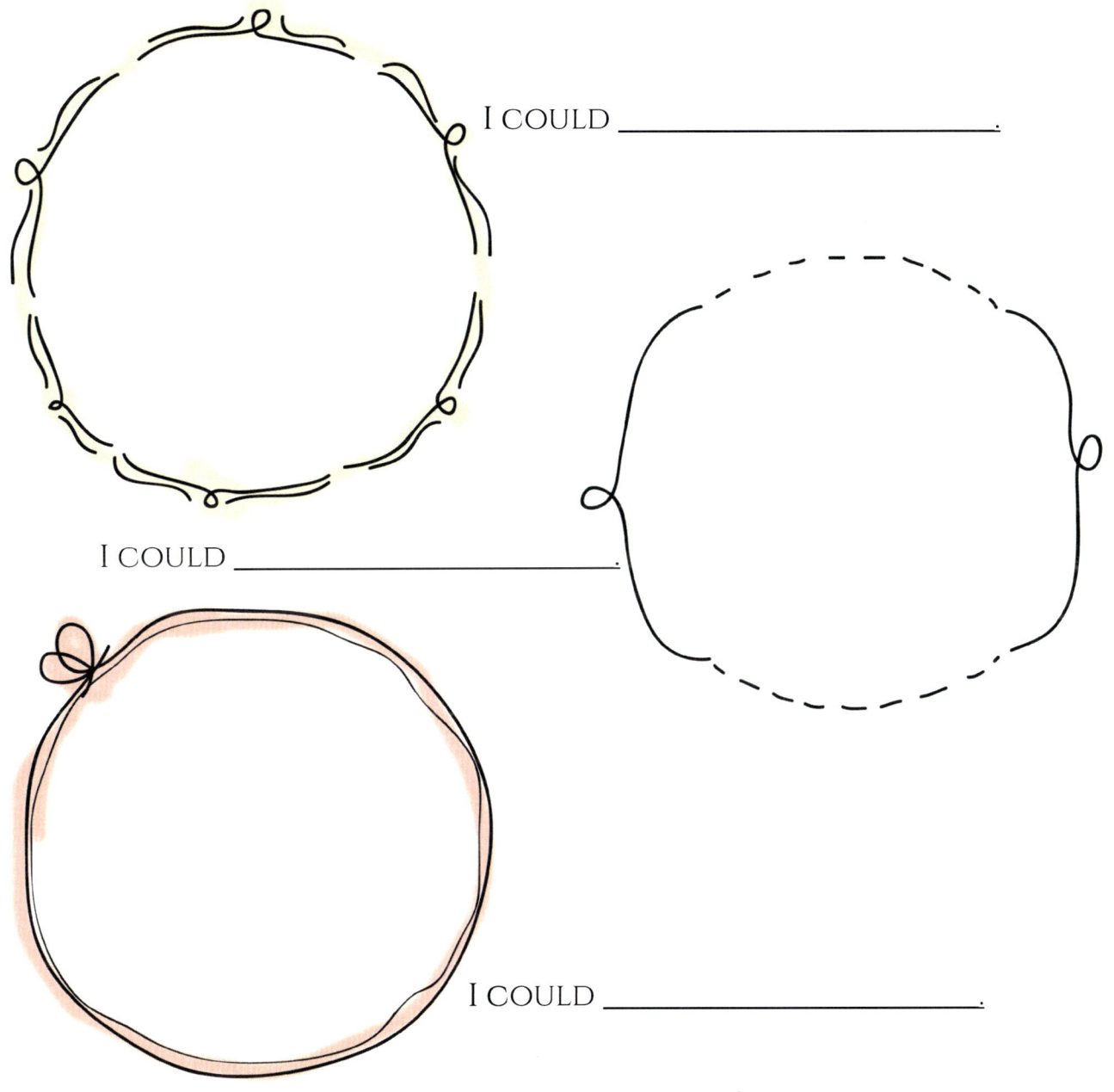

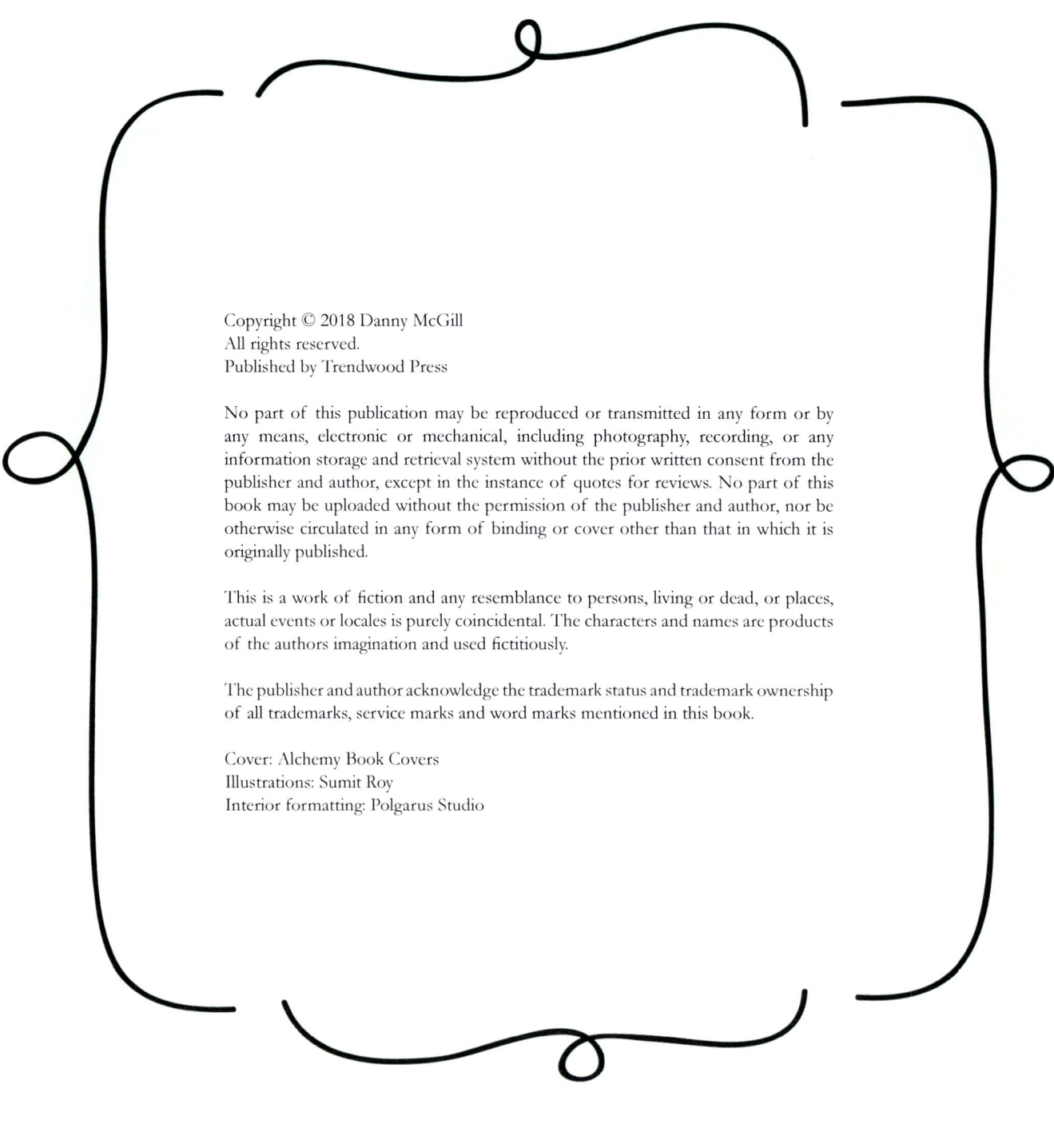

Copyright © 2018 Danny McGill
All rights reserved.
Published by Trendwood Press

No part of this publication may be reproduced or transmitted in any form or by any means, electronic or mechanical, including photography, recording, or any information storage and retrieval system without the prior written consent from the publisher and author, except in the instance of quotes for reviews. No part of this book may be uploaded without the permission of the publisher and author, nor be otherwise circulated in any form of binding or cover other than that in which it is originally published.

This is a work of fiction and any resemblance to persons, living or dead, or places, actual events or locales is purely coincidental. The characters and names are products of the authors imagination and used fictitiously.

The publisher and author acknowledge the trademark status and trademark ownership of all trademarks, service marks and word marks mentioned in this book.

Cover: Alchemy Book Covers
Illustrations: Sumit Roy
Interior formatting: Polgarus Studio

## An Important Note for Parents, Guardians, and Mentors

PARENT FOCUS: As a former classroom teacher and a current stay-at-home dad, I truly believe that strengthening the "I won't quit" muscle is essential to developing perseverance and maturing into a successful adult.

However, you and I both know that there comes a time in life when quitting something is exactly what a person needs to do. Some situations are so unhealthy that they make a person miserable at a deep level, and no amount of "sticking with it" is going to do anything more for that person.

So, what are children to do in these situations?

Children should always feel comfortable going to their parents, guardians, and mentors when activities are making them unhappy.

It is a trusted adult's job to help the child figure out whether this occasion calls for perseverance... or the wisdom to humbly quit and move on to a healthier activity.

Good luck in your journey together!

*Danny McGill*

Author of the Teaching Perseverance books

Made in the USA
Lexington, KY
29 March 2018